MY 1ST GRAPHIC NOVEL

DUMP TRUCK DAY

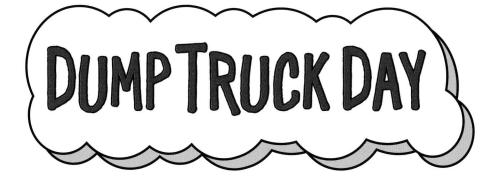

My First Graphic Novels are published by Stone Arch Books
A Capstone Imprint
1710 Roe Crest Drive
North Mankato, Minnesota 56003
www.capstonepub.com

Library of Congress Cataloging-in-Publication Data
Meister, Cari.
Dump truck day / by Cari Meister ; illustrated by Michael Emmerson.
p. cm. — (My first graphic novel)
ISBN 978-1-4342-1621-2 (library binding)
ISBN 978-1-4342-2288-6 (softcover)
1. Graphic novels. [1. Graphic novels. 2. Dump trucks—Fiction. 3. Trucks—Fiction.] I. Emmerson, Michael, ill. II. Title.
PZ7.7.M45Du 2010
741.5'973—dc22

2008053376

Summary: Jacob spends the day riding in a dump truck with his Uncle Kurt.

Creative Director: Heather Kindseth
Graphic Designer: Carla Zetina-Yglesias

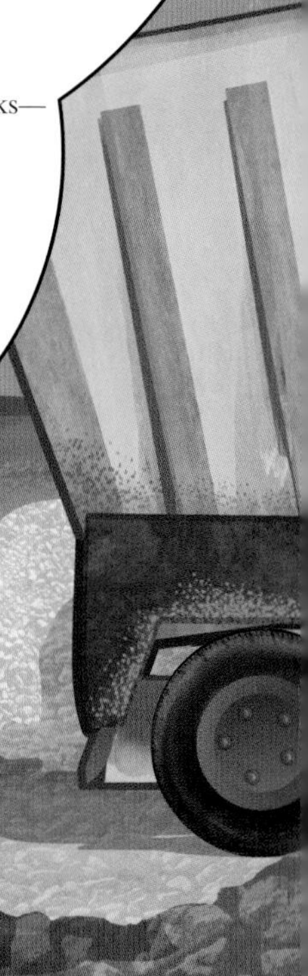

Printed in the United States of America in Stevens Point, Wisconsin.

010654R

MY 1ST GRAPHIC NOVEL

DUMP TRUCK DAY

by Cari Meister
illustrated by Michael Emmerson

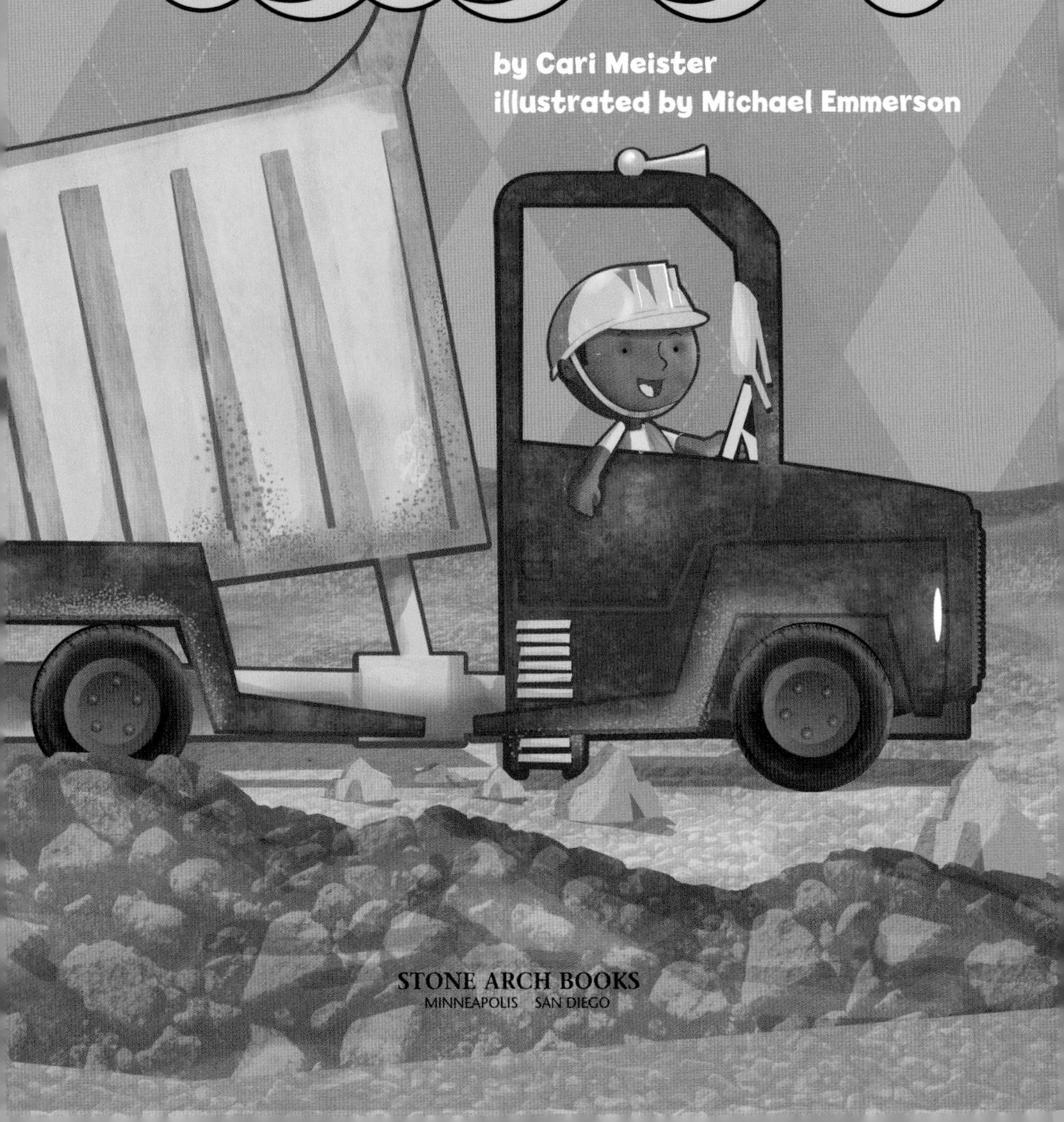

STONE ARCH BOOKS
MINNEAPOLIS SAN DIEGO

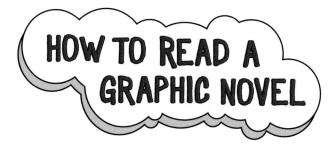

HOW TO READ A GRAPHIC NOVEL

Graphic novels are easy to read. Boxes called panels show you how to follow the story. Look at the panels from left to right and top to bottom.

Read the word boxes and word balloons from left to right as well. Don't forget the sound and action words in the pictures.

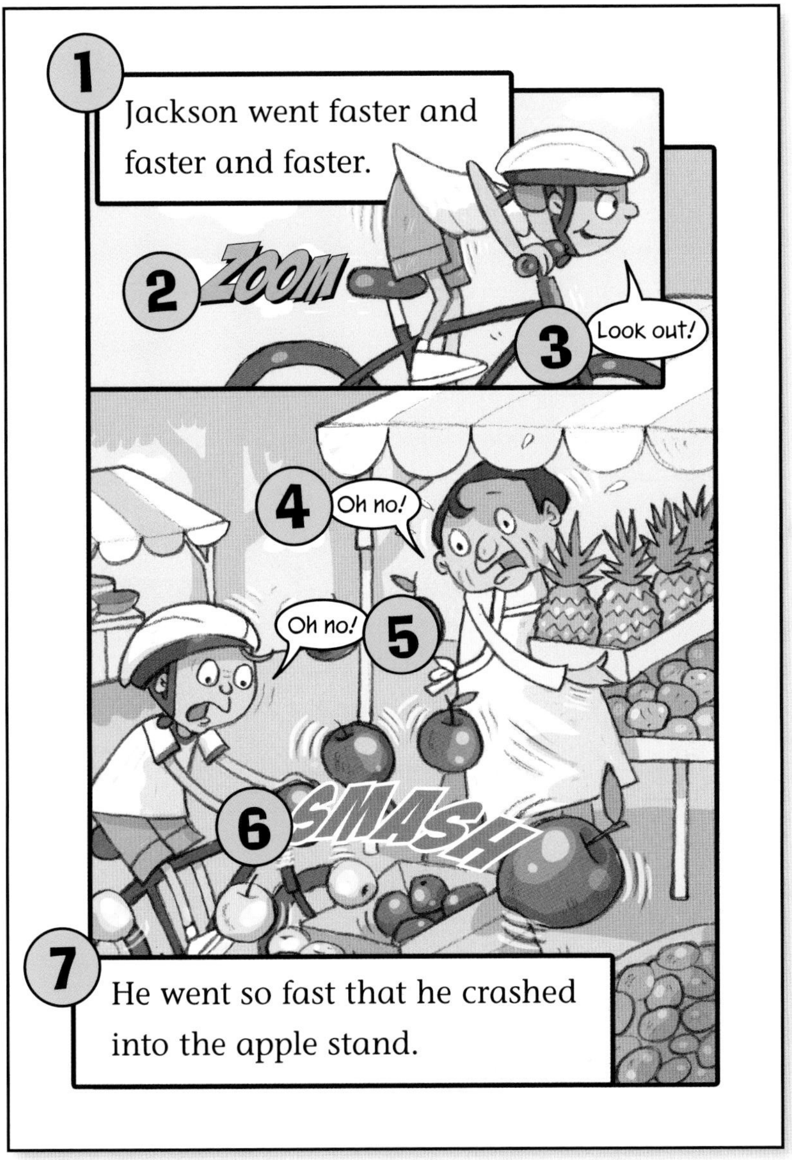
1
Jackson went faster and faster and faster.
2
ZOOM
3
Look out!
4
Oh no!
5
Oh no!
6
SMASH
7
He went so fast that he crashed into the apple stand.

The pictures and the words work together to tell the whole story.

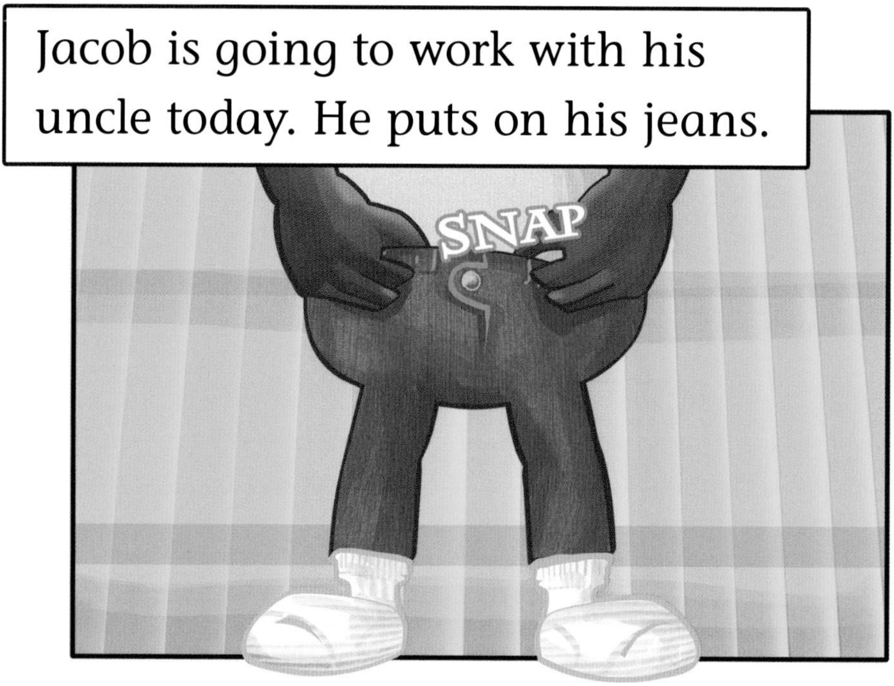
Jacob is going to work with his uncle today. He puts on his jeans.
SNAP

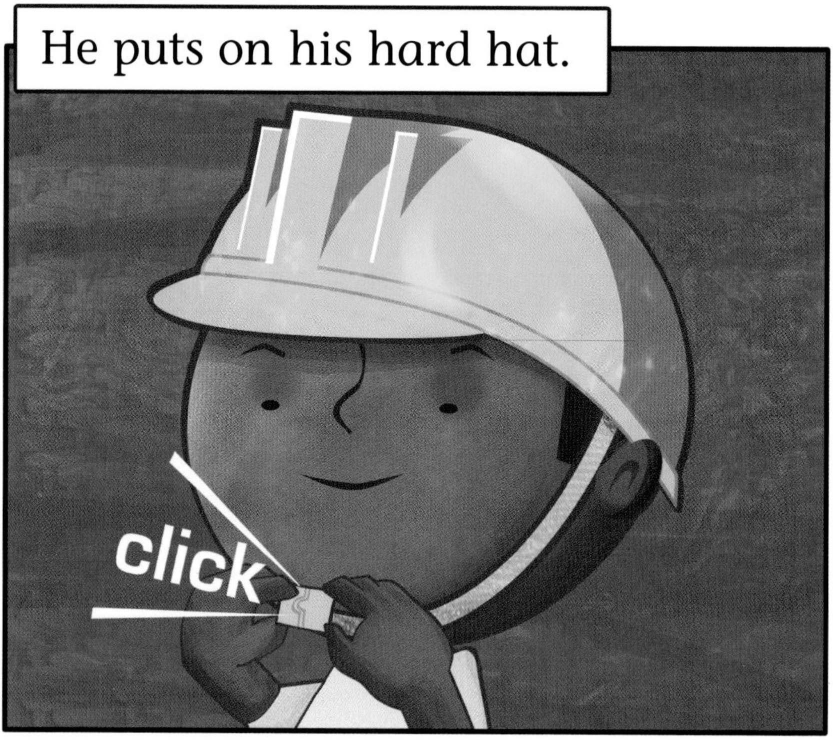
He puts on his hard hat.
click

He puts on his work boots.

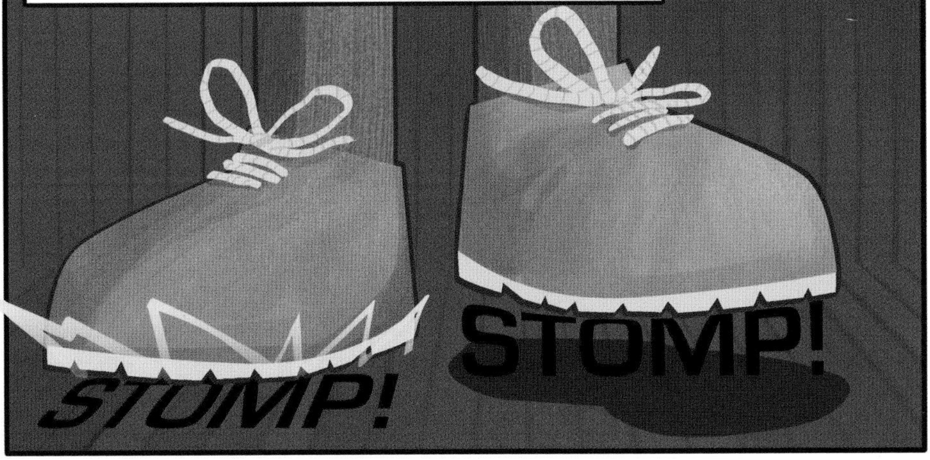
STOMP!
STOMP!

The doorbell rings. It is Uncle Kurt.

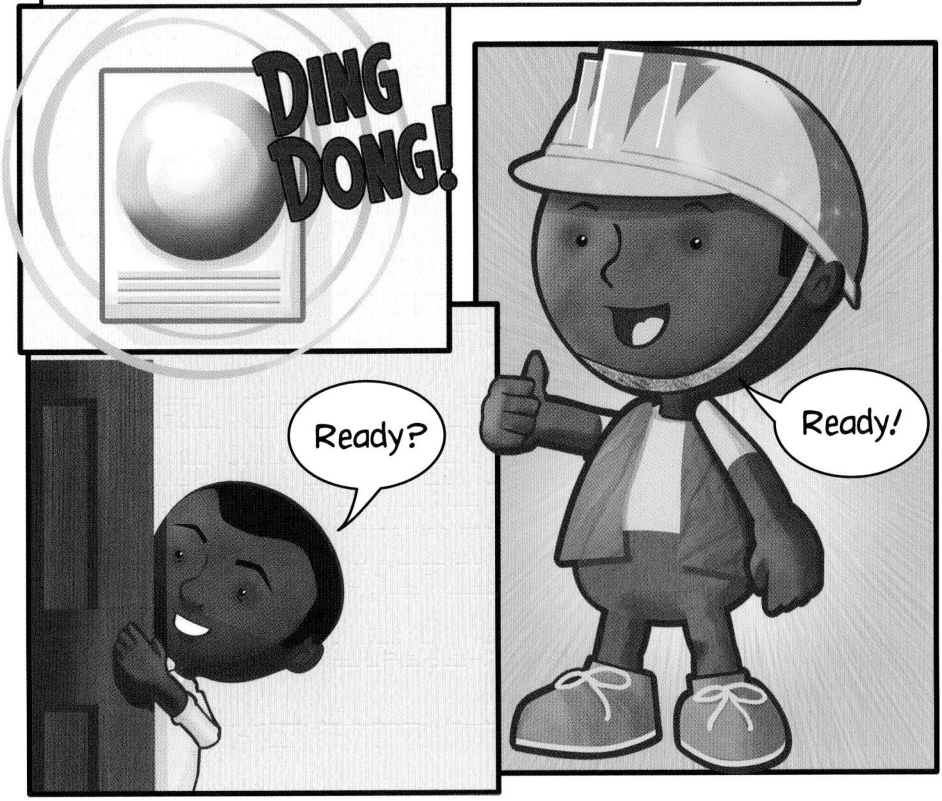
DING DONG!
Ready?
Ready!

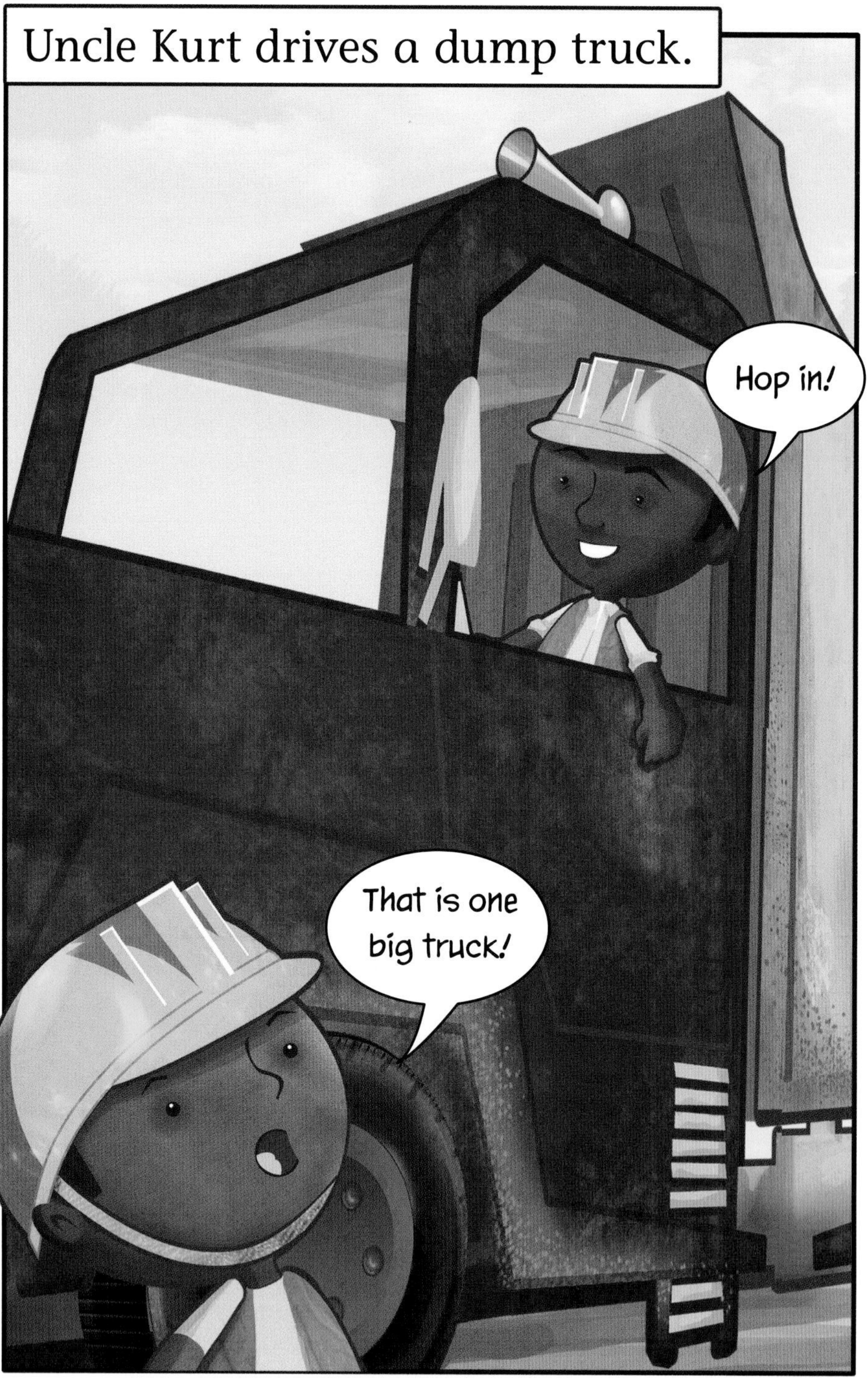
Uncle Kurt drives a dump truck.
Hop in!
That is one big truck!

Uncle Kurt starts the engine.
It is loud.

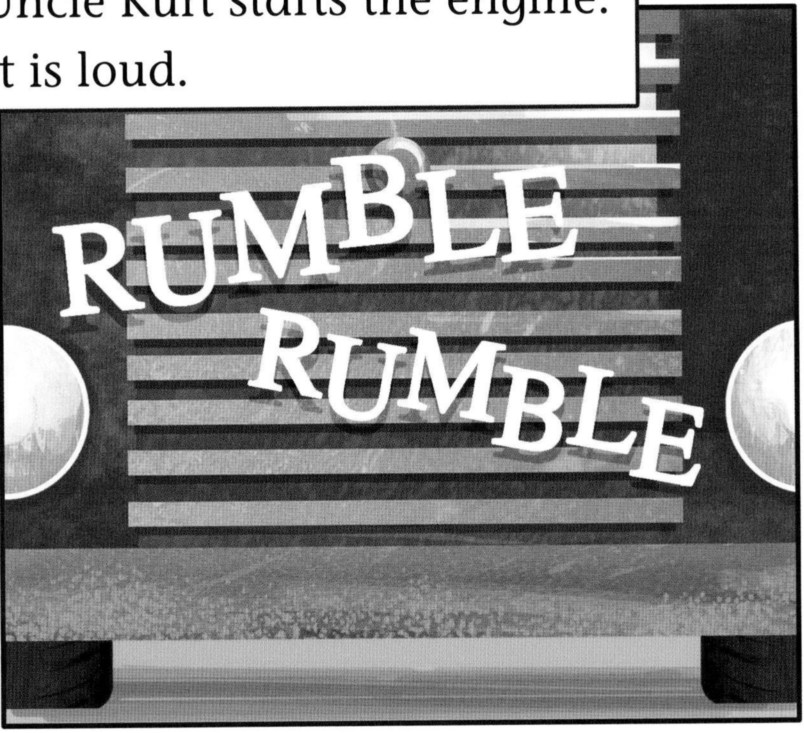
RUMBLE
RUMBLE
RUMBLE

Jacob shuts the heavy door.

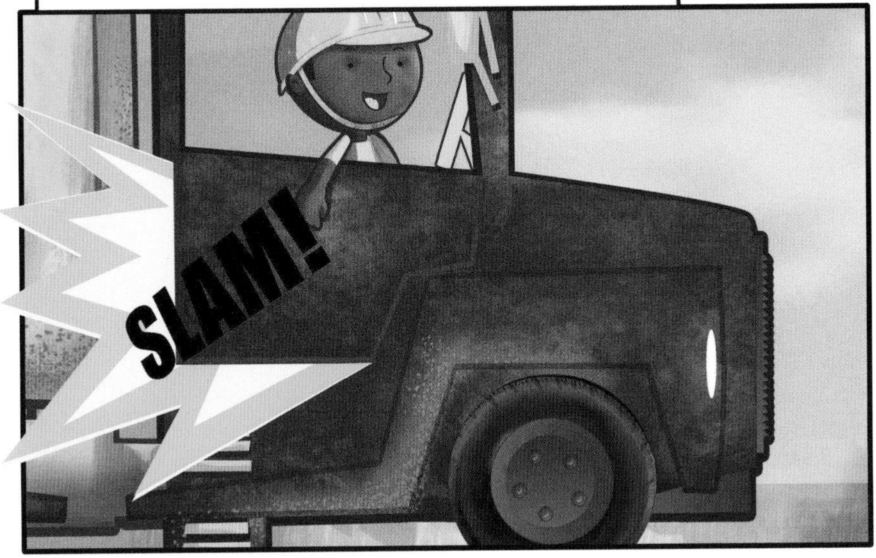
SLAM!

Today they are going to the pit mine.

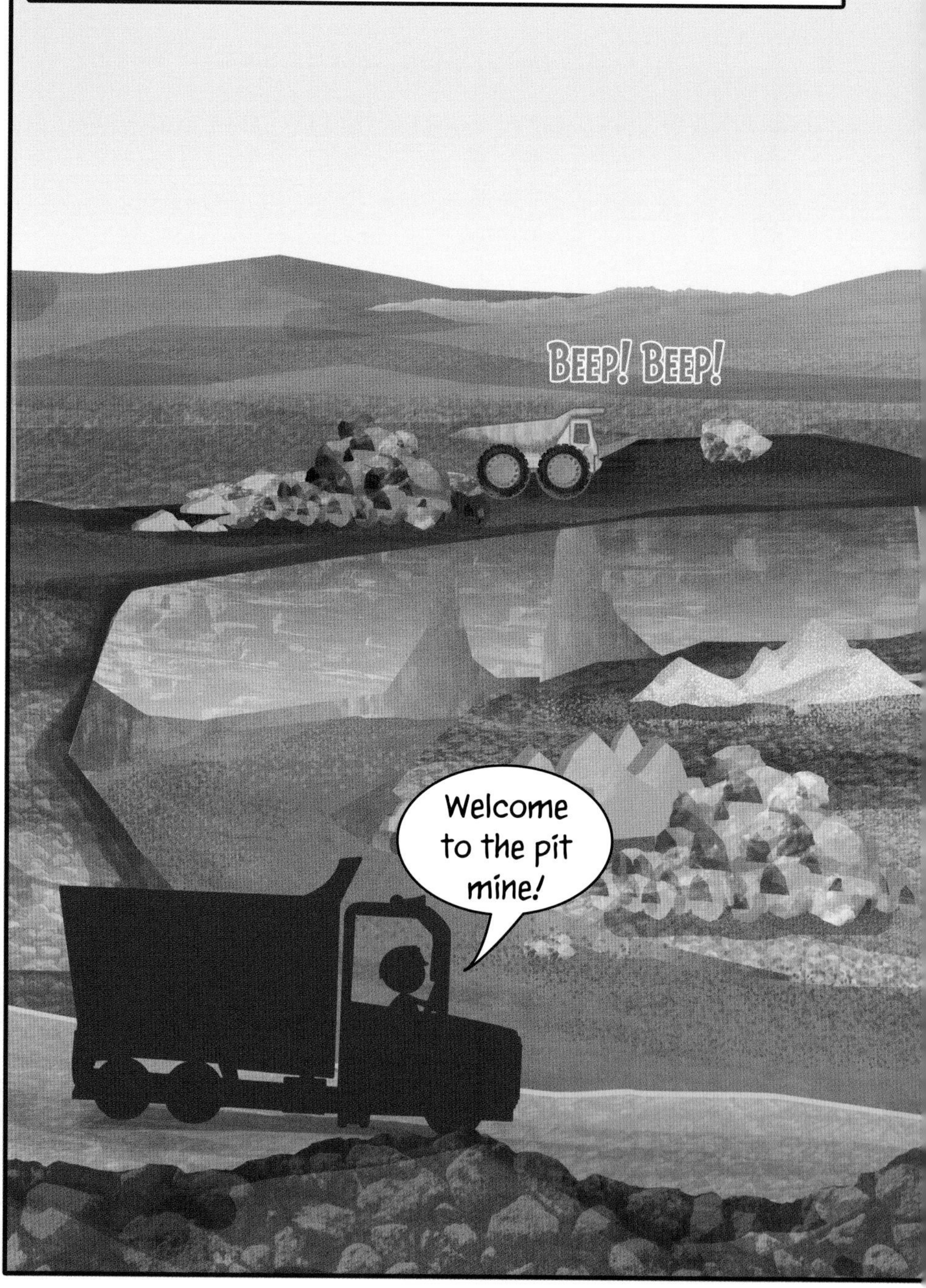
BEEP! BEEP!
Welcome to the pit mine!

The pit mine has mountains of rocks. It has hills of gravel and piles of sand.

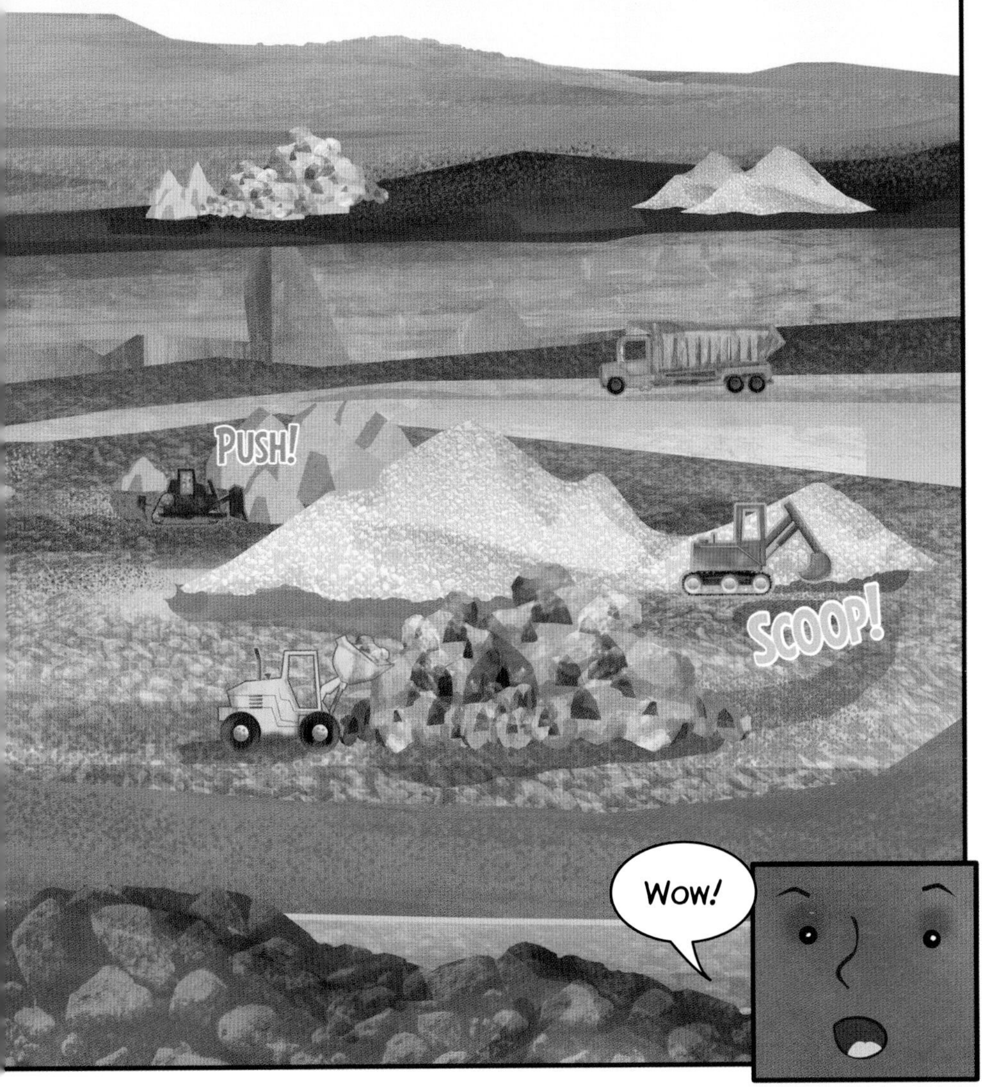
PUSH!
SCOOP!
Wow!

There are all kinds of trucks at the pit mine.

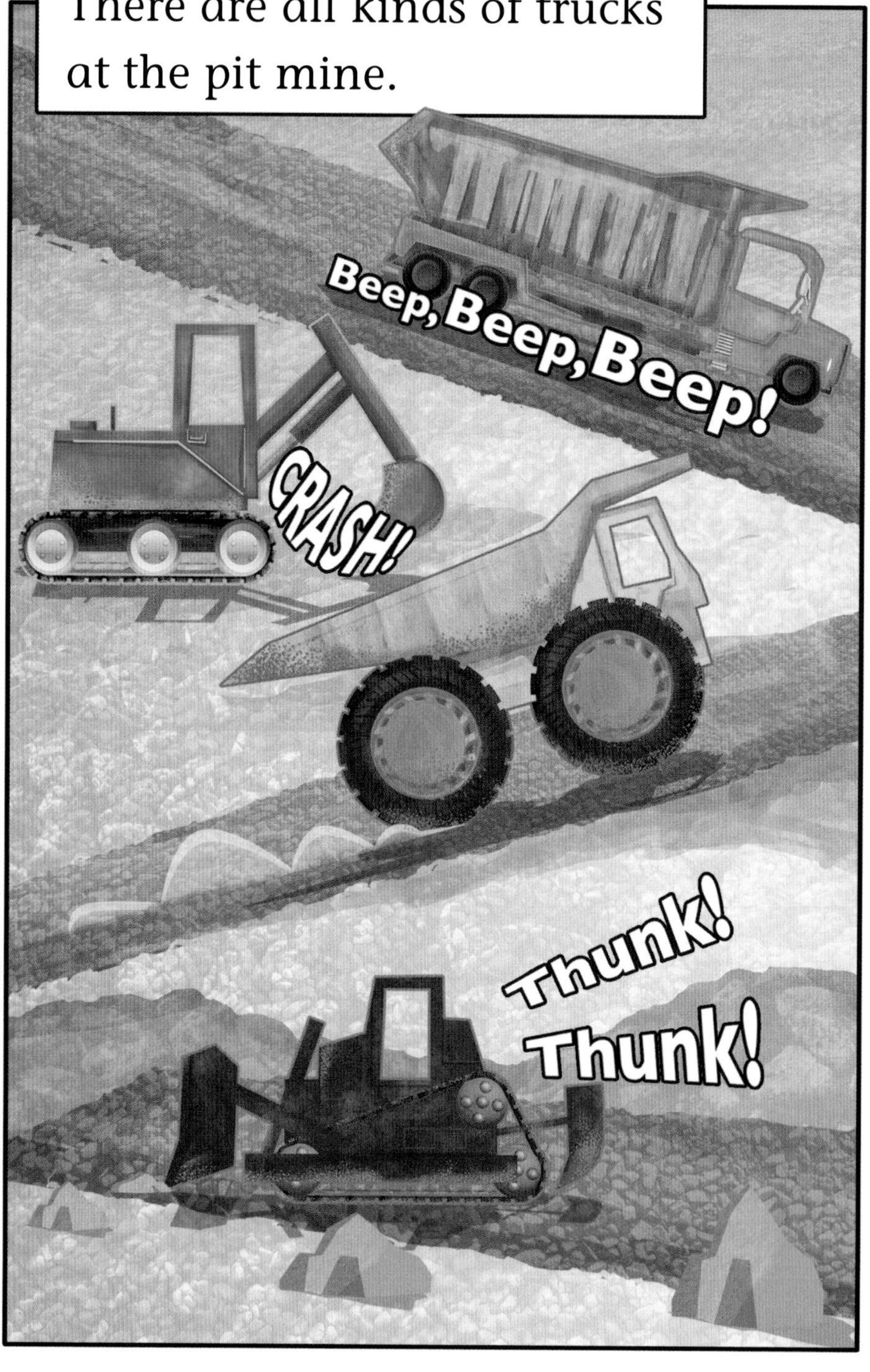
Beep, Beep, Beep!
CRASH!
Thunk!
Thunk!

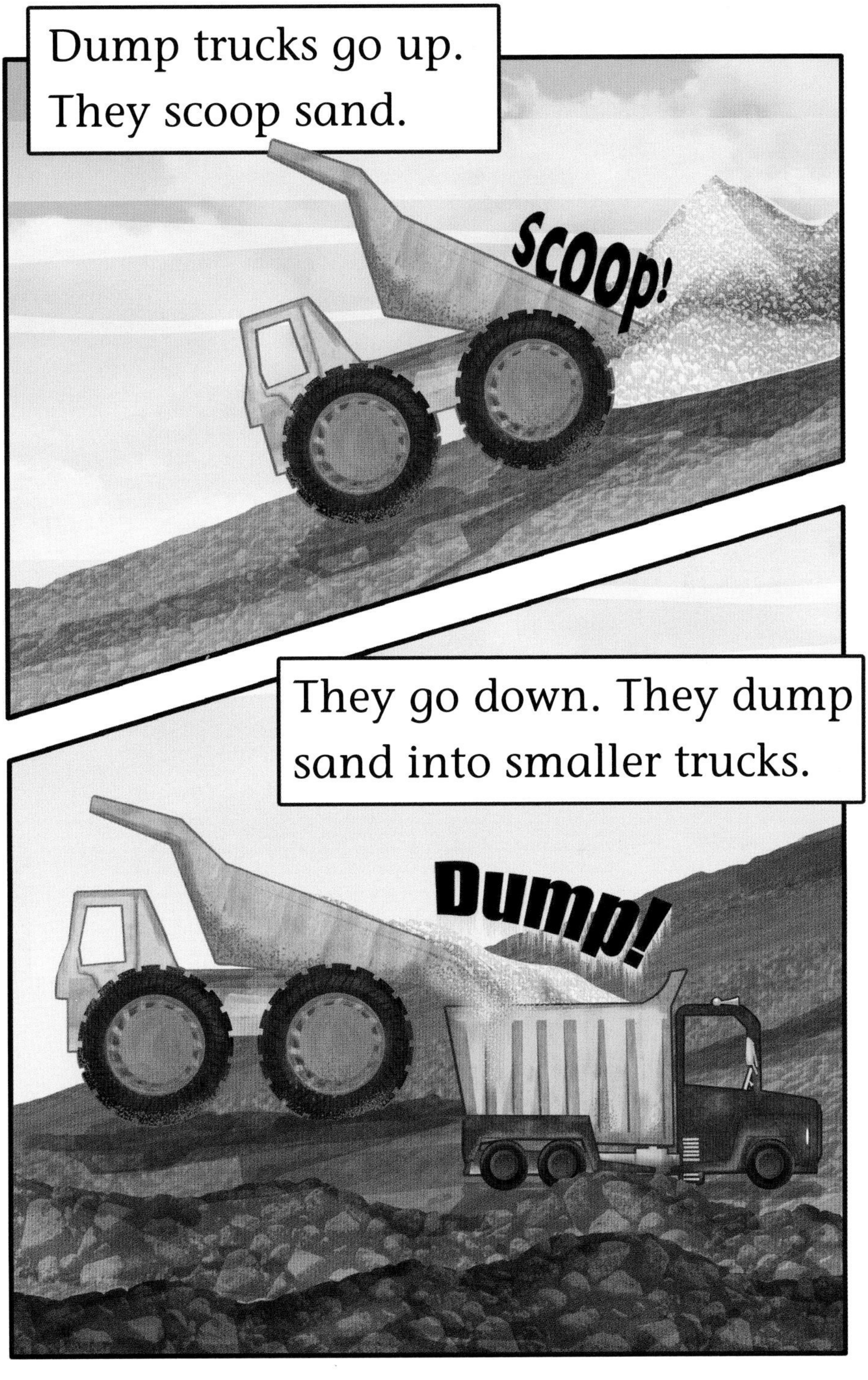
Dump trucks go up. They scoop sand.
SCOOP!
They go down. They dump sand into smaller trucks.
Dump!

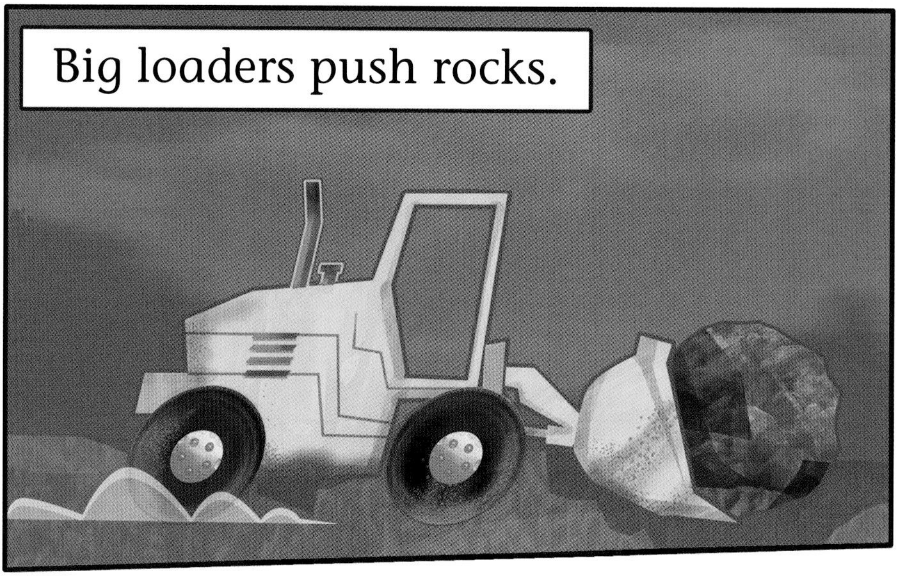
Big loaders push rocks.

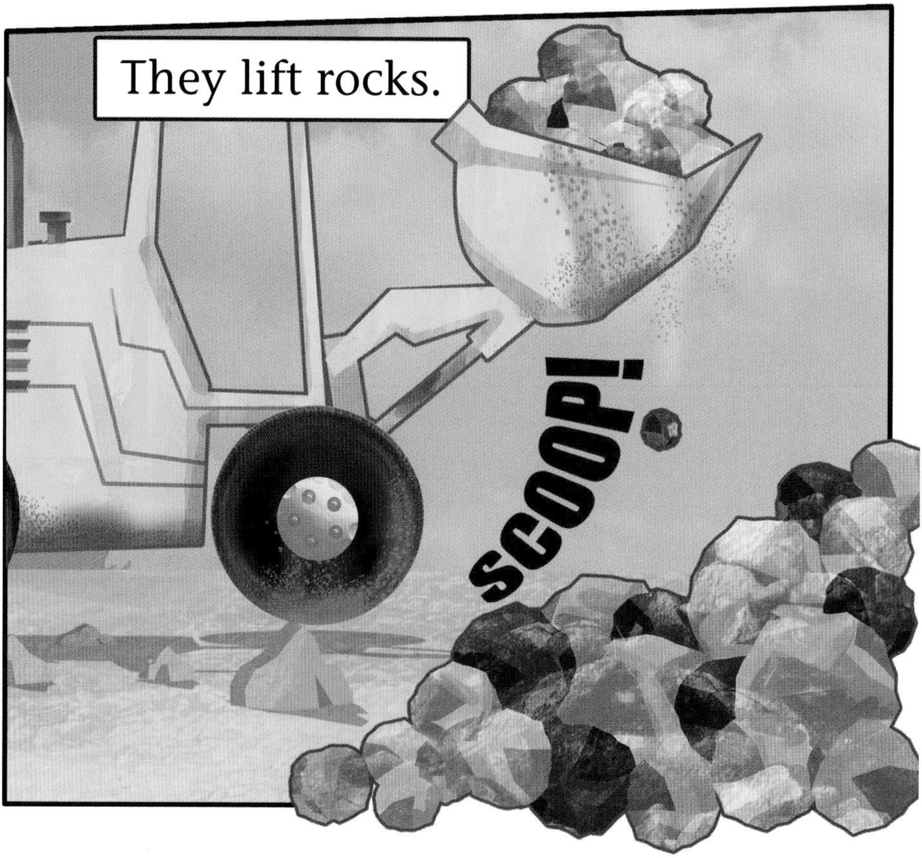
They lift rocks.
SCOOP!

They dump rocks into bigger trucks.

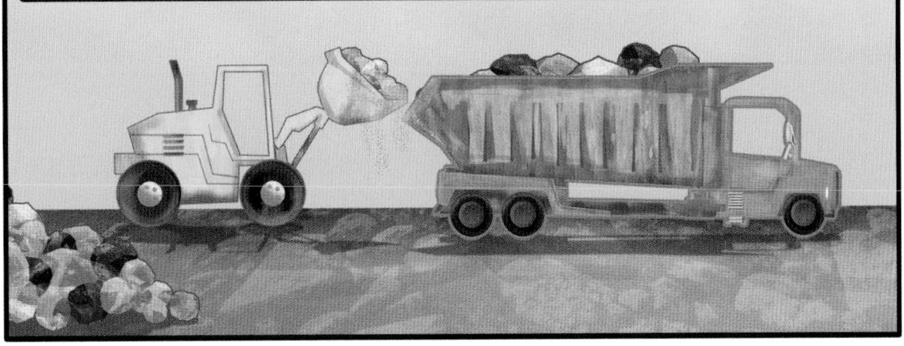

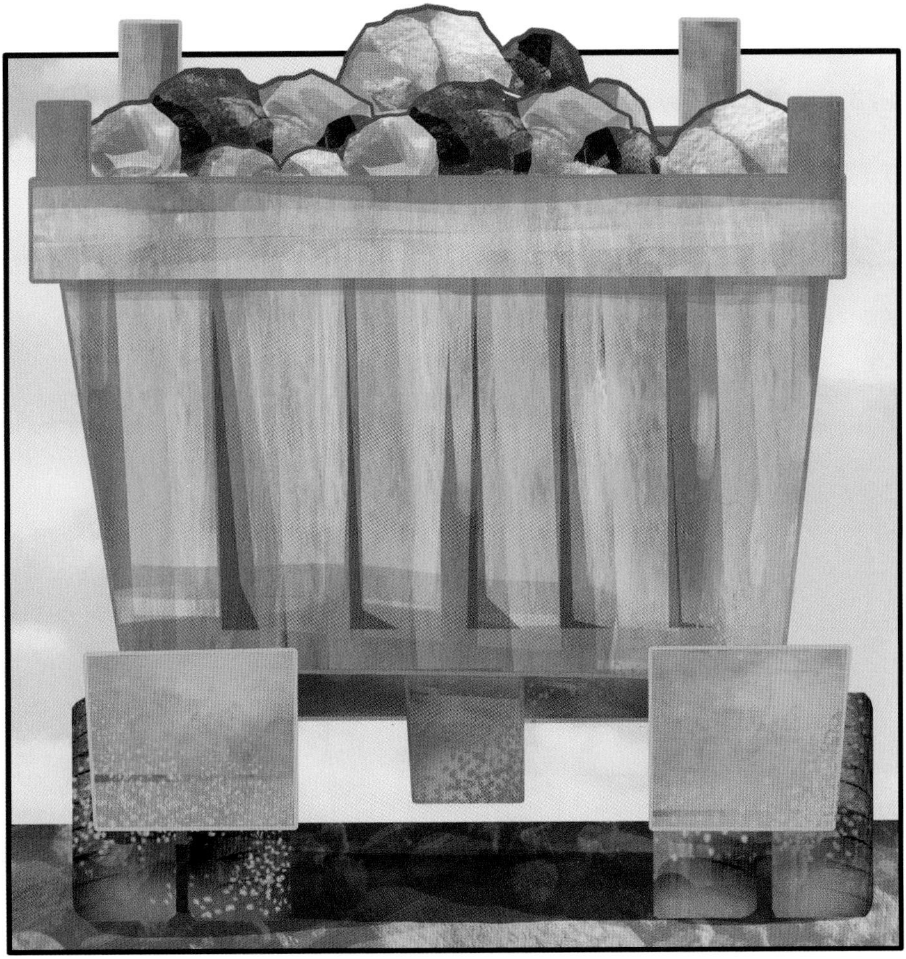

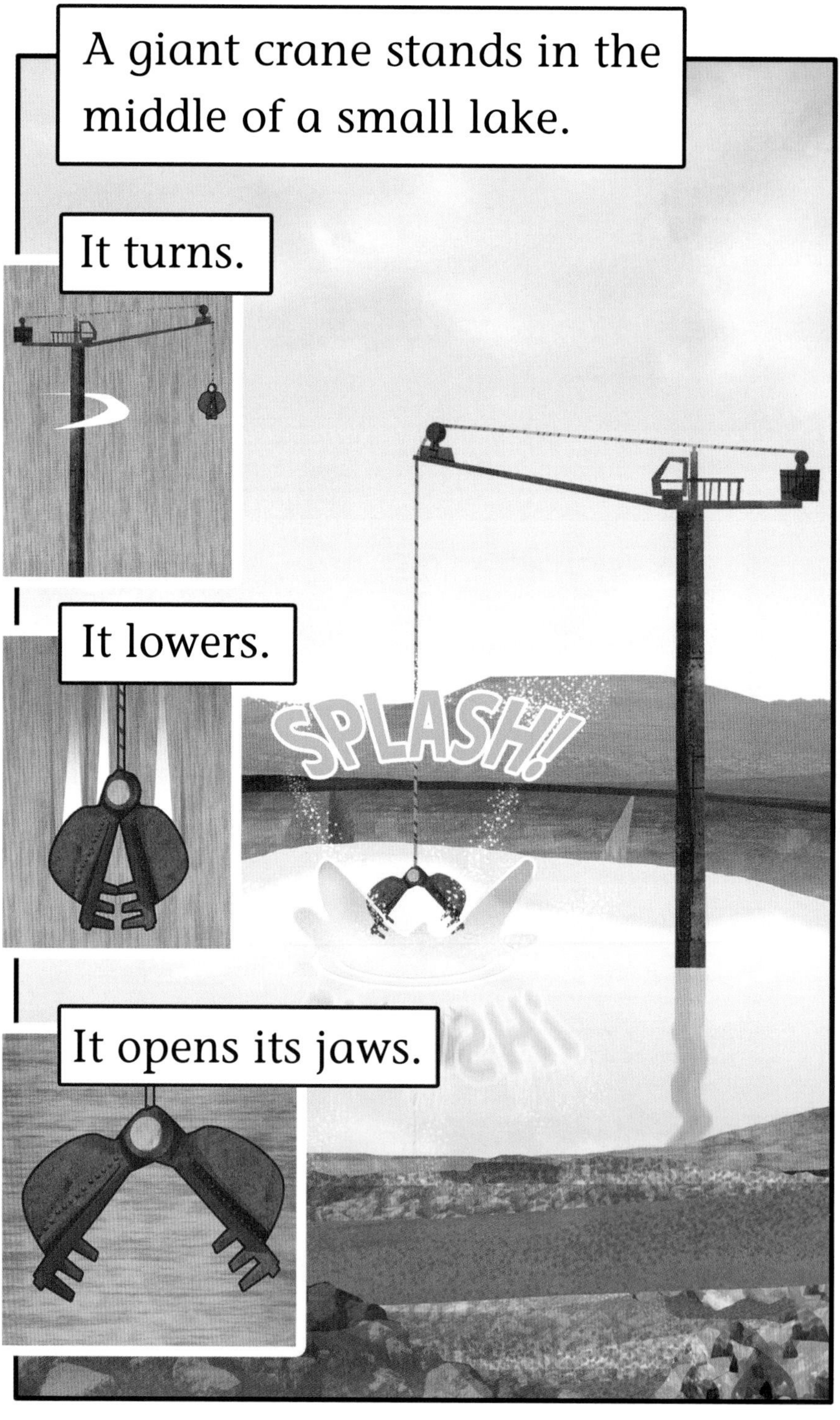
A giant crane stands in the middle of a small lake.
It turns.
It lowers.
SPLASH!
It opens its jaws.

The jaws close under water.

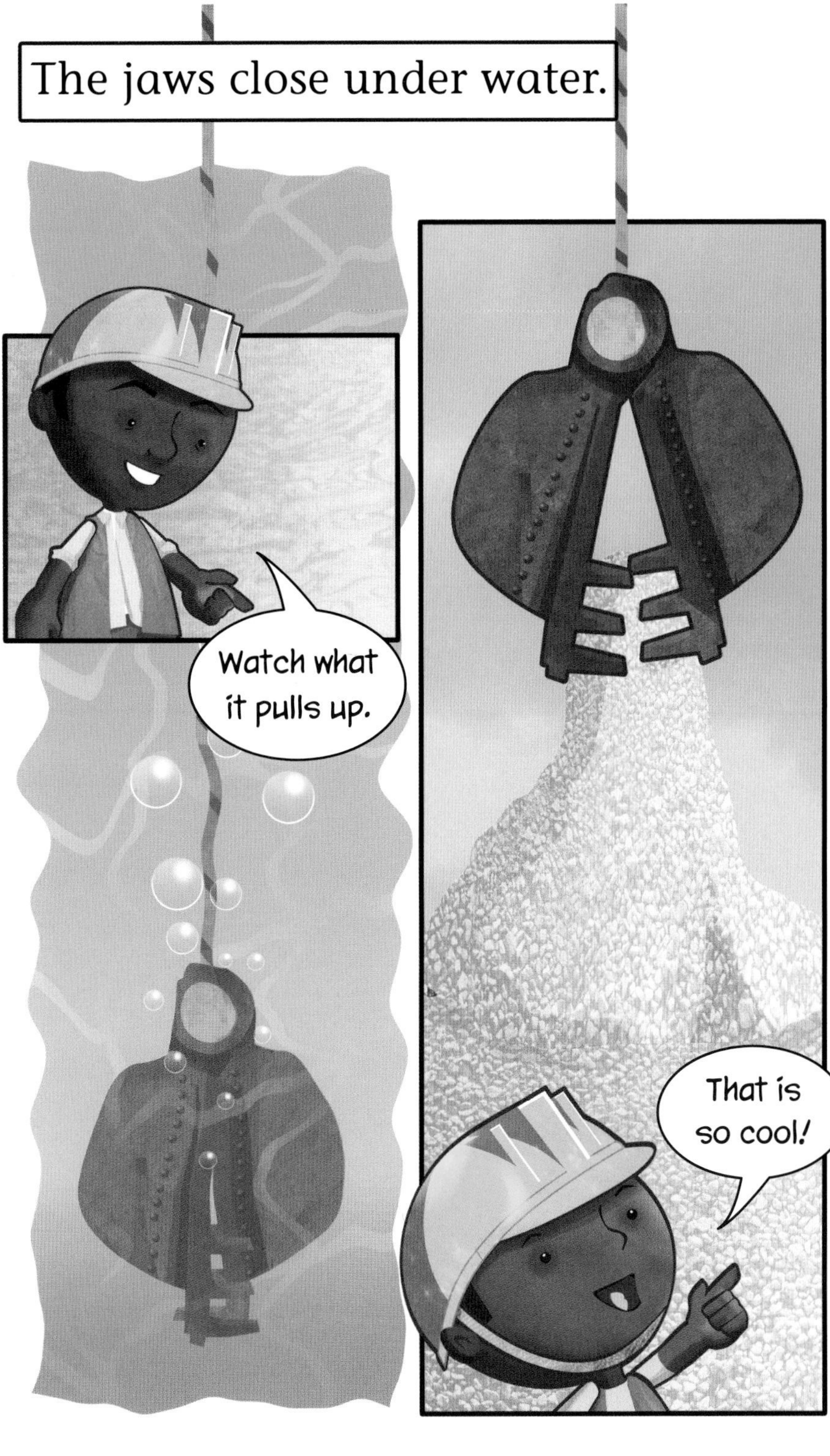
Watch what it pulls up.
That is so cool!

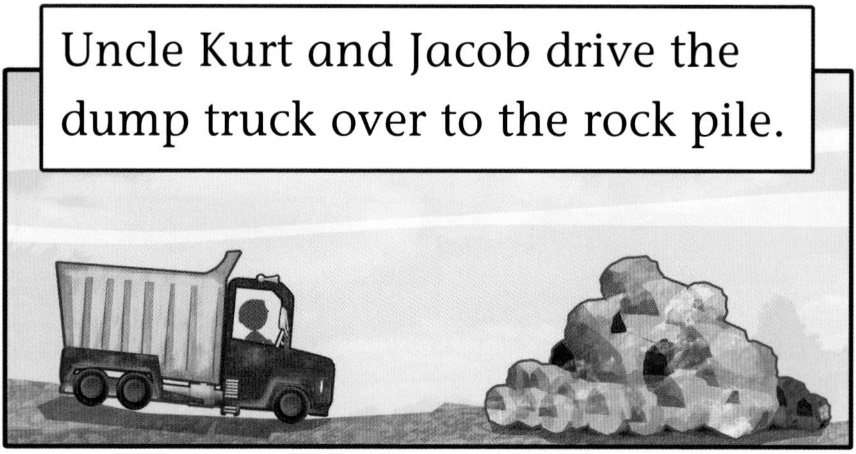
Uncle Kurt and Jacob drive the dump truck over to the rock pile.

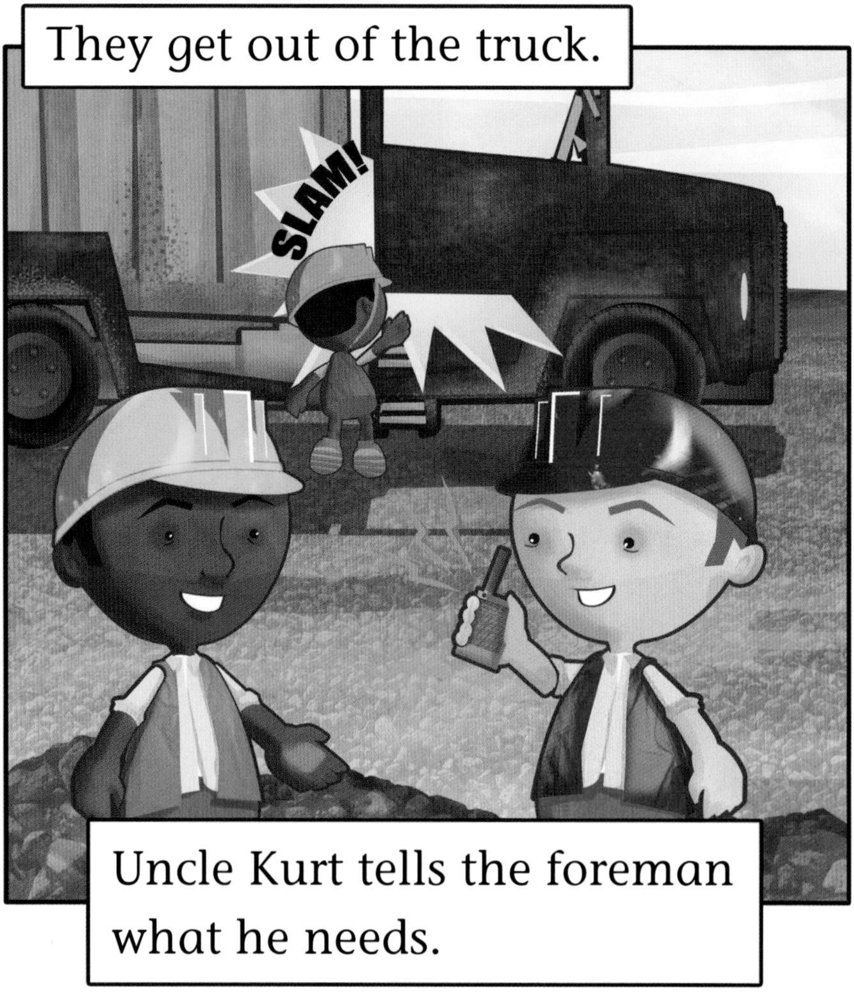
They get out of the truck.
SLAM!
Uncle Kurt tells the foreman what he needs.

A loader comes and pushes.

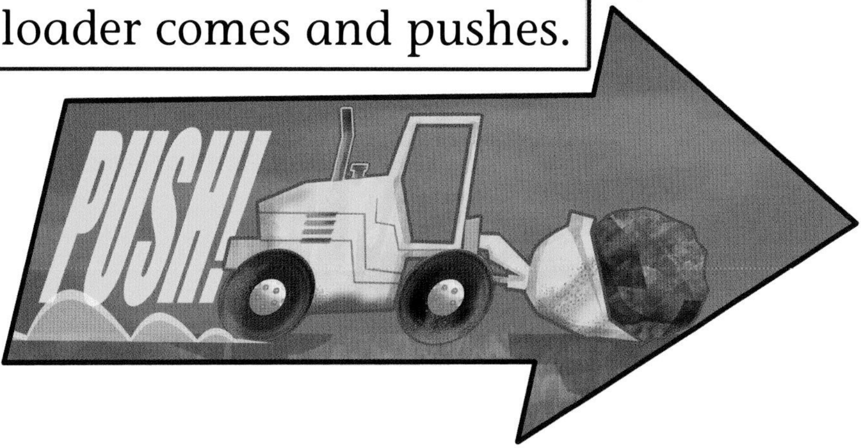
PUSH!

It scoops.

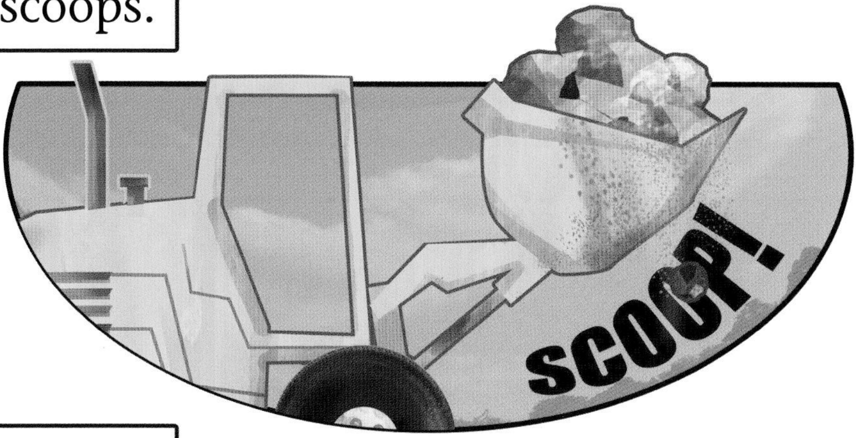
SCOOP!

It dumps.

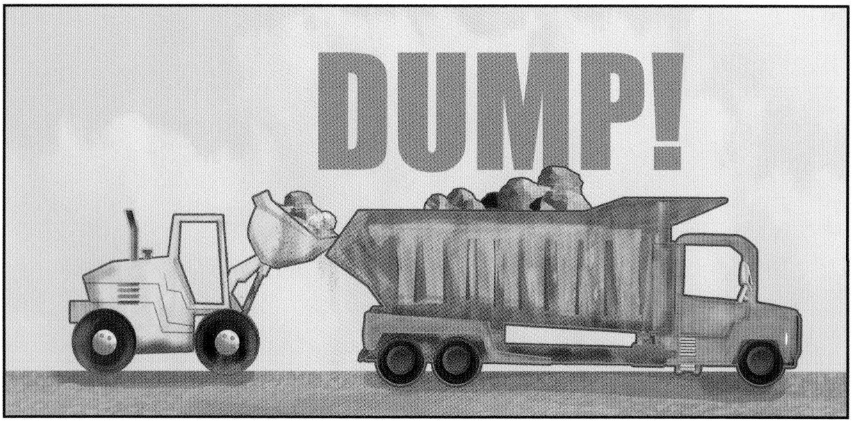
DUMP!

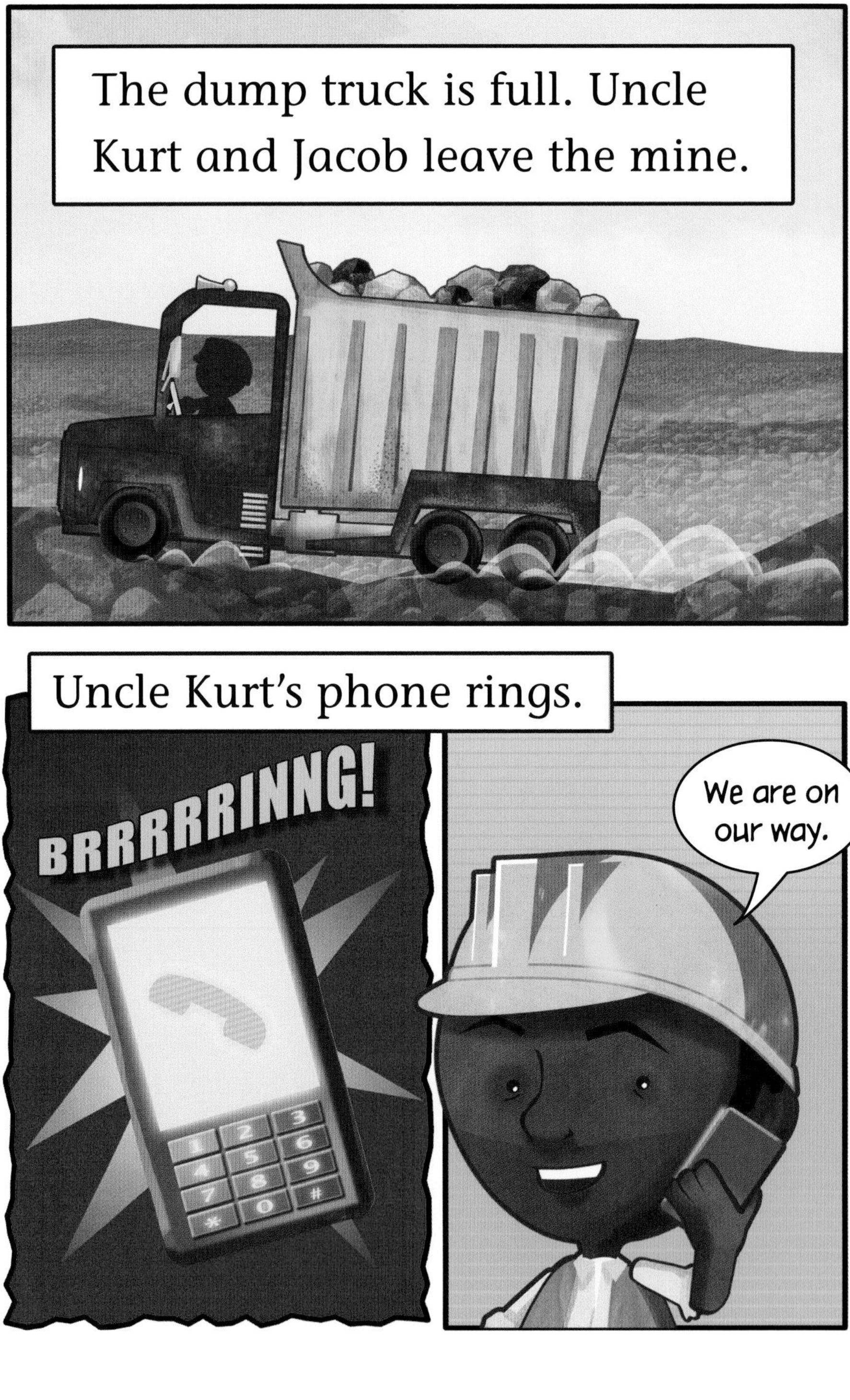
The dump truck is full. Uncle Kurt and Jacob leave the mine.
Uncle Kurt's phone rings.
BRRRRRINNG!
We are on our way.

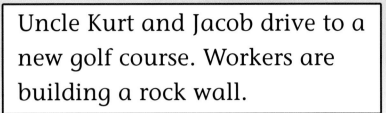

Uncle Kurt and Jacob drive to a
new golf course. Workers are
building a rock wall.

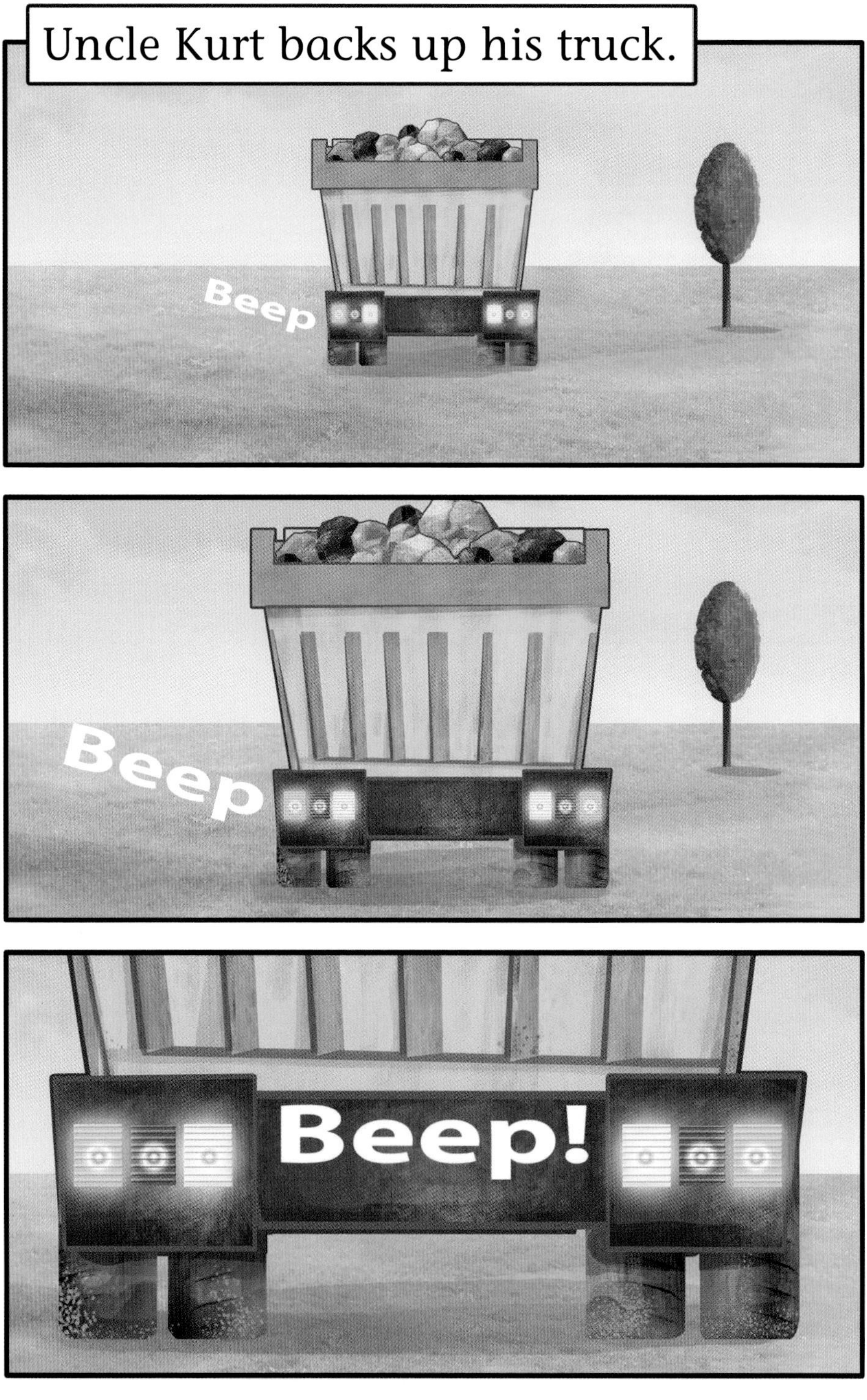
Uncle Kurt backs up his truck.
Beep
Beep
Beep!

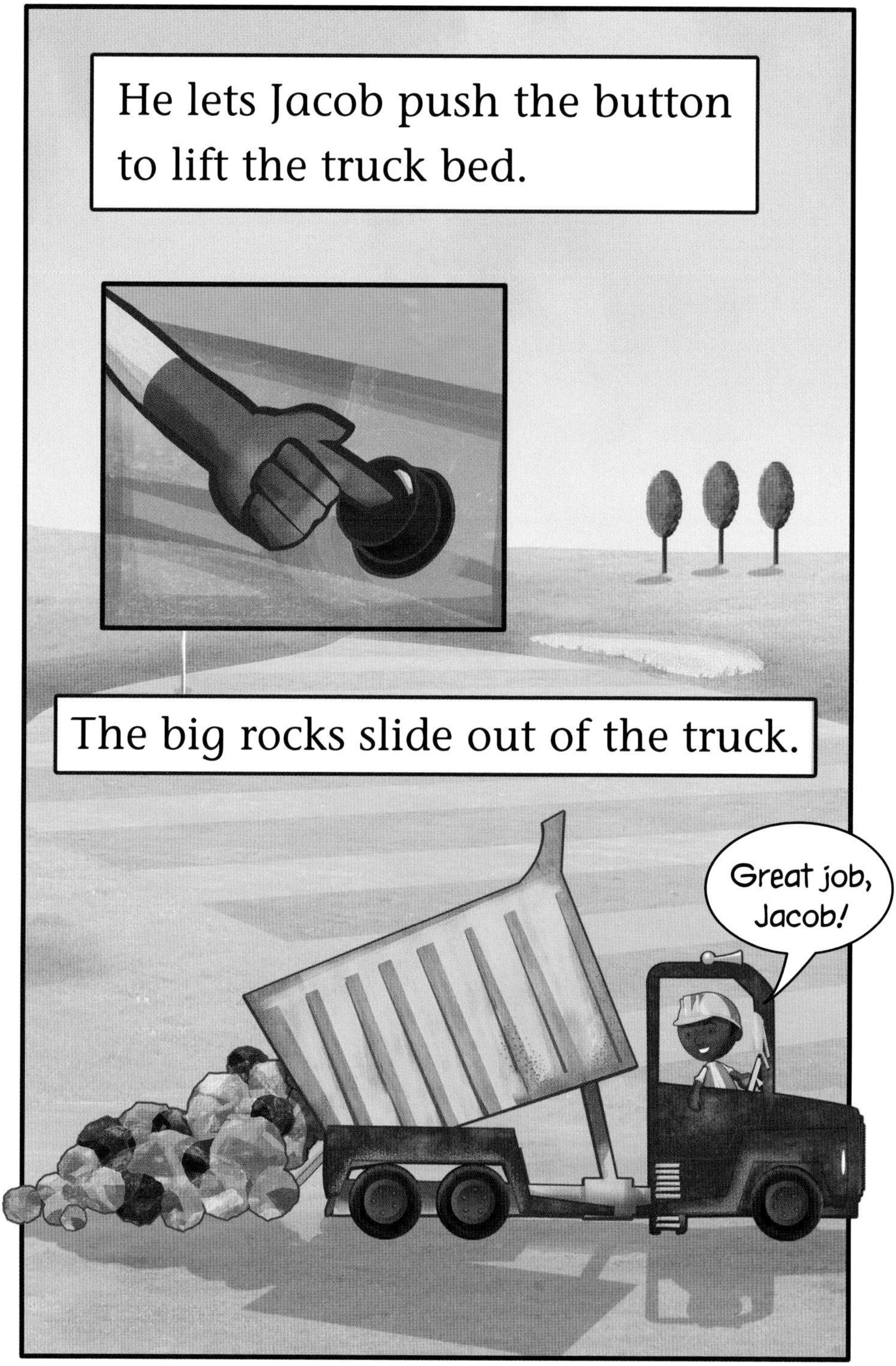
He lets Jacob push the button to lift the truck bed.
The big rocks slide out of the truck.
Great job, Jacob!

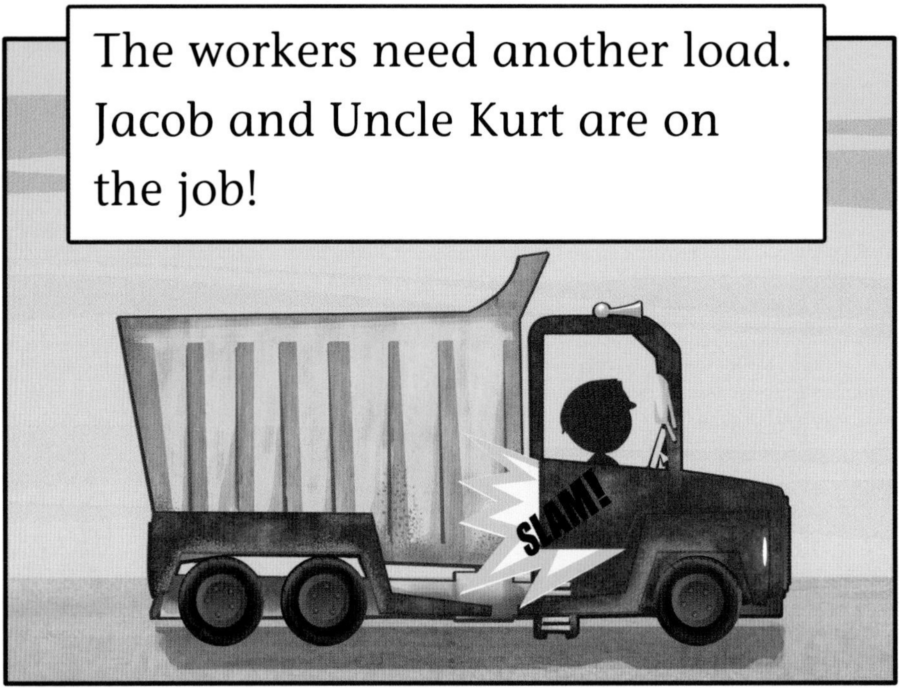
The workers need another load. Jacob and Uncle Kurt are on the job!
SLAM!

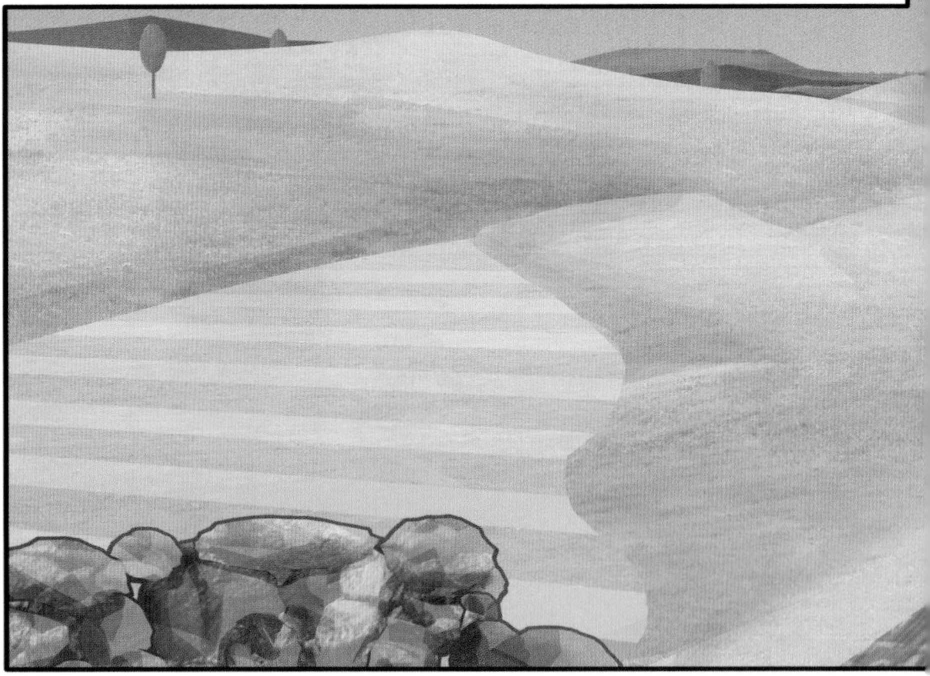

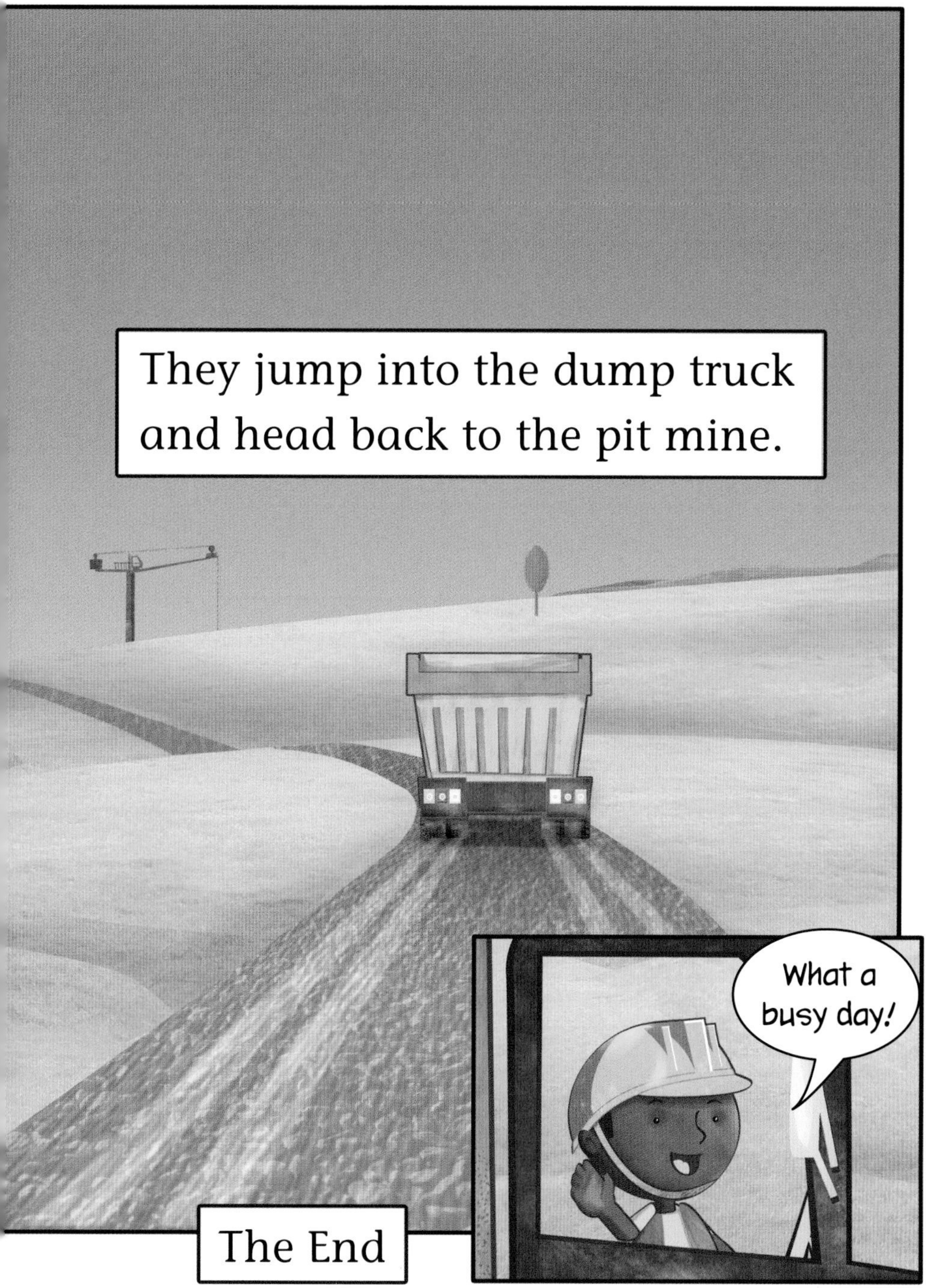
They jump into the dump truck and head back to the pit mine.
What a busy day!
The End

ABOUT THE AUTHOR

Cari Meister is the author of many books for children, including the My Pony Jack series and *Luther's Halloween*. She lives on a small farm in Minnesota with her husband, four sons, three horses, one dog, and one cat. Cari enjoys running, snowshoeing, horseback riding, and yoga. She loves to visit libraries and schools.

ABOUT THE ILLUSTRATOR

Michael Emmerson has been drawing pictures ever since he could pick up a burnt sienna crayon and scribble all over the wallpaper. Now he uses pencils, paper, and a computer. He lives in the suburbs of London with his lovely wife, Alice. When he's not drawing pictures or solving mysteries, he also designs toys, video games, and chocolates.

crane (KRANE)—a machine with a long arm that lifts heavy objects

engine (EN-juhn)—the part of a vehicle that makes it move

foreman (FOR-muhn)—the person in charge of a work area

gravel (GRAV-uhl)—a type of dirt that has small stones in it

jaws (JAWZ)—the part of a machine used to grab an object or objects

loader (LOHD-ur)—a vehicle with a scoop in front for digging and loading material

DISCUSSION QUESTIONS

1.) Would you like to drive a big truck? Why or why not?

2.) Jacob's uncle is a dump truck driver. What kind of job do you want when you get older?

3.) Jacob's uncle wears a hard hat for safety. Why is it important to wear safety gear for certain jobs?

WRITING PROMPTS

1.) There are many different trucks in this story. Draw a picture of the truck you would like to drive.

2.) Draw a map of the pit mine in the story. Make sure to include the lake, the boulder mountains, the sand hills, and the road.

3.) Throughout the book, there are sound and action words next to some of the pictures. Pick at least two of those words. Then write your own sentences using those words.

MY 1ST GRAPHIC NOVEL

THE 1ST STEP INTO GRAPHIC NOVELS

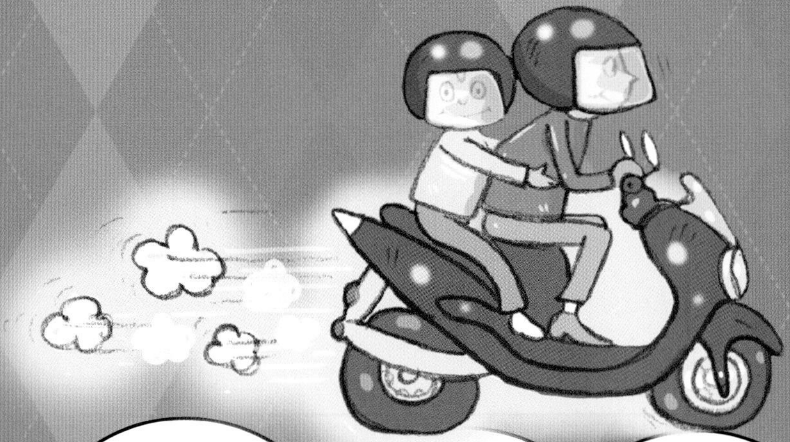

These books are the perfect introduction to graphic novels. Combine an entertaining story with comic book panels, exciting action elements, and bright colors, and a safe graphic novel is born.

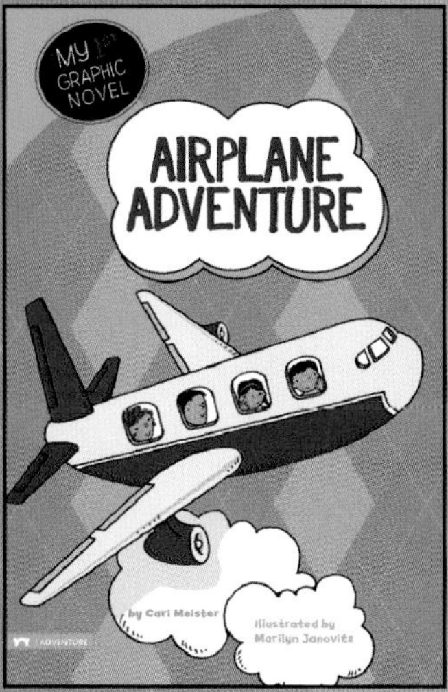
MY 1ST GRAPHIC NOVEL
AIRPLANE ADVENTURE
by Cari Meister
illustrated by Marilyn Janovitz

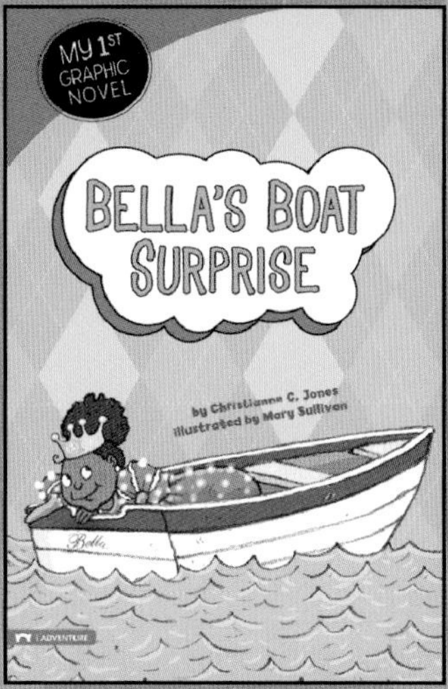
MY 1ST GRAPHIC NOVEL
BELLA'S BOAT SURPRISE
by Christianne C. Jones
illustrated by Mary Sullivan

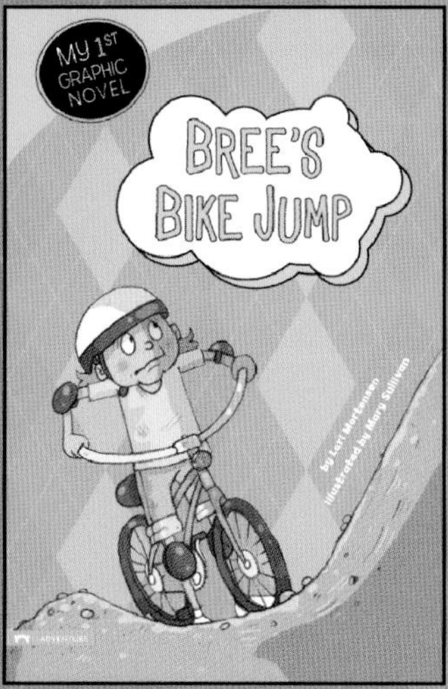
MY 1ST GRAPHIC NOVEL
BREE'S BIKE JUMP
by Lori Mortensen
illustrated by Mary Sullivan

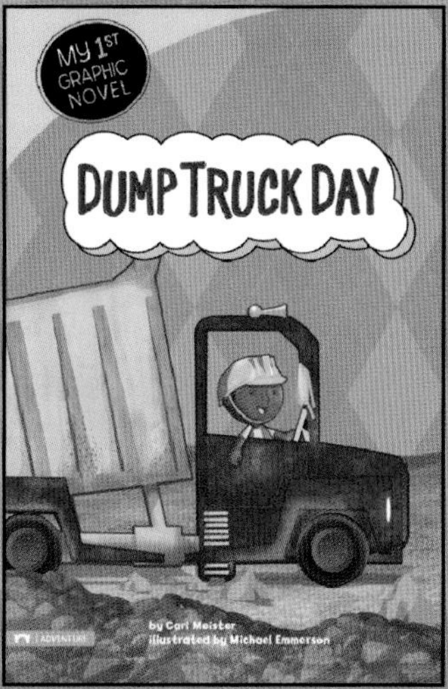
MY 1ST GRAPHIC NOVEL
DUMP TRUCK DAY
by Cari Meister
illustrated by Michael Emmerson

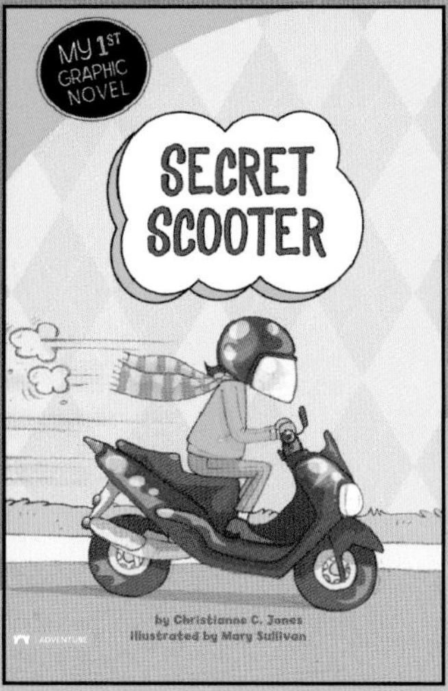
MY 1ST GRAPHIC NOVEL
SECRET SCOOTER
by Christianne C. Jones
illustrated by Mary Sullivan

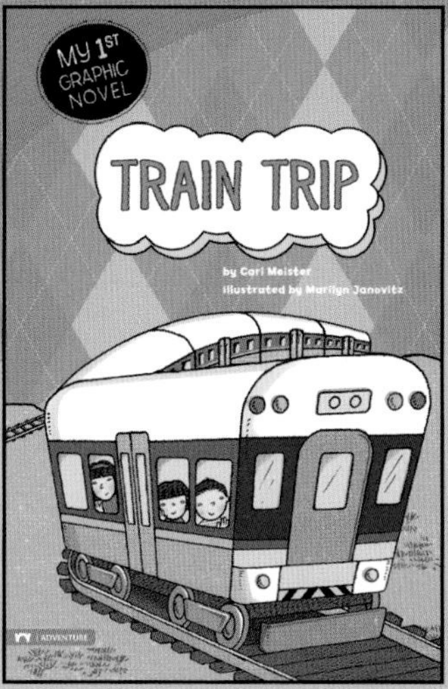
MY 1ST GRAPHIC NOVEL
TRAIN TRIP
by Cari Meister
illustrated by Marilyn Janovitz